Click, Clack, PEEP!

Click, Clack, Peep!

Doreen Cronin
Illustrated by Betsy Lewin

Atheneum Books for Young Readers
New York London Toronto Sydney New Delhi

For Betsy and Ted
—D. C.

For little Ellis,
the newest "peep" in the Lewin clan
—B. L.

Click, Clack, peep!

Farmer Brown stuck his head out the window.
The farm was too quiet.
Everyone was watching the egg.

Not a moo.   Not an oink.
Not a click.   Not a clack.

Not a baa.
Not a cluck.
Not a thing.

Then . . . a crack.

Inside the barn
everyone gathered closer.

moo?

crack

baa?

crack

Baby Duck!

Baby Duck laughed.
PEEP PEEP PEEP
And laughed again.

Baby Duck waddled.
PEEP PEEP PEEP
And waddled again.

Baby Duck played.
PEEP PEEP PEEP
And played again!

The animals yawned.

peep peep peep

And yawned again.

The chickens sang a lullaby.

But Baby Duck would not sleep.

peep
peep
peep

The cows lowered the shades.

But Baby Duck would not sleep.

peep peep peep

The sheep knitted a blanket.

But Baby Duck would not sleep.

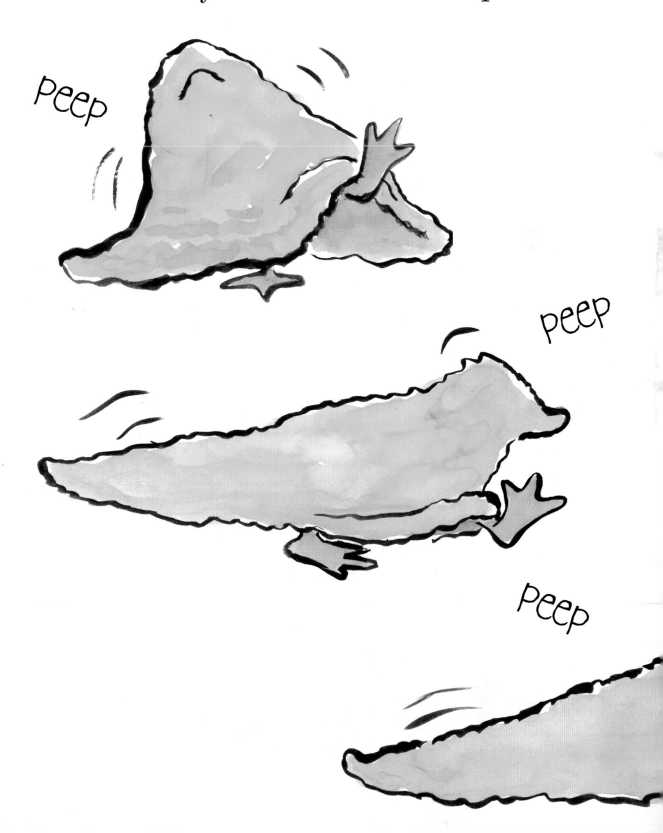

The chickens went outside to get some sleep.
The cows went outside to get some sleep.

The sheep went outside to get some sleep.
The mice went outside to get some sleep.

Duck took off his headphones.

peep
peep
peep

He put Baby Duck
into a bucket.

peep peep peep

He covered her
with a blanket.

peep peep peep

He carried her
outside.

peep peep peep

He climbed
into
the tractor.

peep peep peep

He buckled up the seat belts.

peep peep peep

And backed out of the barnyard.

beep beep beep

He drove
back and forth.

peep
peep
peep

Back and forth.

peep peep peep

Back and forth.

peep, peep . . .

...*sleep.*

Farmer Brown opens his eyes
after a good night's sleep.

Not a moo.
Not a cluck.
Not a clack.

Not a peep.